Absolutely Lucy

by Ilene Cooper
illustrated by Amanda Harvey

A STEPPING STONE BOOK™
Random House 🏠 New York

For the real Emmelou and her boy, Bill —I.C.

To Michael —A.H.

This is a work of fiction. Names, characters, places, and incidents either are the product of the author's imagination or are used fictitiously. Any resemblance to actual persons, living or dead, events, or locales is entirely coincidental.

Text copyright © 2000 by Ilene Cooper
Interior illustrations copyright © 2000 by Amanda Harvey
Cover illustration copyright © 2004 by Mary Ann Lasher

All rights reserved. Published in the United States by Random House Children's Books, a division of Random House, Inc., New York.

Random House and the colophon are registered trademarks and A Stepping Stone Book and the colophon are trademarks of Random House, Inc.

Visit us on the Web!
SteppingStonesBooks.com
www.randomhouse.com/kids

Educators and librarians, for a variety of teaching tools, visit us at
www.randomhouse.com/teachers

The Library of Congress has cataloged the first Random House edition of
this book as follows:
Cooper, Ilene.
Absolutely Lucy / by Ilene Cooper ; illustrated by Amanda Harvey.
    p.   cm.
"A Stepping Stone Book."
Summary: Bobby is a shy boy until he gets a beagle puppy named Lucy, who
helps him to make new friends.
ISBN 978-0-307-26502-9 (pbk.) — ISBN 978-0-307-46502-3 (lib. bdg.)
[1. Bashfulness—Fiction. 2. Beagle (Dog breed)—Fiction. 3. Dogs—Fiction.]
I. Harvey, Amanda, ill. II. Title. III. Series.
PZ7.C7856Ab 2004   [E]—dc22   2003014987

Printed in the United States of America
25 24 23 22

Random House Children's Books supports the First Amendment and
celebrates the right to read.

Contents

Shy Guy

Bobby Quinn did not have any friends. He was shy. He had been shy as long as he could remember.

He was very shy when he was three years old. His relatives came to the Quinns' house for Thanksgiving that year.

Bobby ran into his bedroom and crawled under his bed.

"Bobby, come out and say hello," his mother begged.

Nobody could make him come out.

Bobby was very shy when he was five years old. On the first day of kindergarten, Bobby cried. He didn't want his mother to leave. He didn't want to meet the children in his class.

"But Bobby," his mother said, "don't you want to make new friends?"

"Absolutely not!" Absolutely was the biggest word Bobby knew. He used it whenever he could.

Bobby cried every day for a month. When he stopped crying, it was too late. By then, none of the children wanted to meet him. They called him Cry Bobby.

Bobby was very shy in the first grade. He was shy in the second grade, too. He kept his head down. He didn't look up, even when the teacher called on him.

After school, Bobby did his homework. He spent the rest of his time drawing. He was good at drawing. He drew dinosaurs and fast cars.

When second grade was over, Mrs. Quinn wanted Bobby to go to camp.

"Absolutely not!" Bobby said.

"But what will you do all day?" Mrs. Quinn asked.

"I'll read. I'll draw," Bobby answered.

Mrs. Quinn sighed. "That sounds a little lonely."

Bobby didn't think it sounded lonely. He thought it sounded great. He was very happy when his parents said he didn't have to go to camp.

One hot day in July, Bobby was sitting at his desk. He was drawing a big dinosaur with lots of spikes on its back. His mother came into the room.

"It's such a nice day," she said. "Why don't you go out and play?"

"I don't want to," Bobby said. He didn't

look up from his drawing.

His mother tried again. "Have you seen the new children who moved in across the street? They're setting up a volleyball net. Shall we go introduce ourselves?"

Bobby just shook his head no.

"Bobby, if you don't try to be friendly, you'll never have any friends. Doesn't that bother you?" Mrs. Quinn asked.

"I don't need friends," Bobby whispered as his mother closed the door behind her.

But when he was alone in his room, he put his pencil down and looked out the window. What he said to his mother wasn't really true. He would like to make a friend. He just didn't know how.

2
The Birthday Present

Bobby's eighth birthday came in the middle of July. His parents invited the relatives over for a party in the backyard.

Bobby had three cousins. Ryan and Brian were twelve-year-old twins. They didn't pay too much attention to Bobby. His cousin Jenny was only four. She paid too much attention to Bobby. She followed him wherever he went.

Jenny and her mother and father were the first to arrive for the party. Bobby went outside. Jenny was right behind him. She watched him throw a ball against the side of the garage.

"Mommy's having a baby," Jenny said.

"I know," Bobby answered.

"That's why she's getting so fat. She's as fat as a pig, don't you think?"

Bobby frowned. "That's not a very nice thing to say, Jenny."

Jenny looked surprised. "It isn't? But I love pigs."

Bobby didn't know what to say to that.

"Bobby, do you like your birthday?"

"Absolutely," Bobby answered.

"What does that word mean?" Jenny asked.

Bobby stopped throwing the ball. He thought for a minute. "Absolutely means yes. A real big, big yes. But if you say absolutely not, that means a real big no."

"Why do you always say it?"

Bobby shrugged.

"I like the way it feels on my tongue."

Jenny tried to say it. "Ab-see-loot-ee."

"No," Bobby corrected. "Absolutely."

She tried again. "Ab-silly-oot-ly."

Bobby gave up. "Maybe you'll be able to say it next year, Jenny."

Bobby started throwing his ball against the garage again.

"Hey, Bobby," Jenny said, "I know what your mommy and daddy are giving you for your birthday."

Bobby caught the ball. "You do?"

Jenny nodded.

"Tell me. What am I getting?"

Jenny put her hands over her mouth. She tried to keep the surprise inside. But she was so excited, the words burst out anyway.

"An eagle!"

"An eagle?" Bobby was shocked. "I'm getting an eagle?"

Jenny nodded her head hard. "I heard Mommy telling Daddy."

"But an eagle is a bird," Bobby said. "A big bird."

Jenny nodded again. "Mommy said it would be nice for you to have a pet."

Bobby plunked himself down on the driveway. A pet? He had a pet once. A turtle. It crawled behind the washing machine. Bobby never saw it again.

He didn't do a very good job of taking care of the turtle. How could he take care of an eagle?

Bobby had read about eagles in school. The eagle was the symbol of the United States because it was strong and proud. Maybe his parents wanted him to be strong and proud, too.

Jenny tugged at Bobby's shirt. "What's the matter? You don't like eagles?"

"I like them okay." He thought about his small room. "But they are so big."

"It's a baby eagle," Jenny told him.

"How do you know that?"

"Mommy saw it. She said it was cute and small. And soft."

Well, that sounded like a baby eagle. But baby eagles grow. Didn't his parents know that?

Brian and Ryan arrived with their parents. They let Bobby play a game of three-way catch with them. They were being nice because it was his birthday.

"Do you know what I'm getting for my birthday?" Bobby asked.

Brian and Ryan looked at each other.

"We're not supposed to tell," Ryan said.

"It's a surprise," Brian said.

"I don't like surprises."

"Okay, we're giving you a book," Brian said.

"About dinosaurs," Ryan added.

"Have you heard anything about a bird?" Bobby asked.

"You mean, like a parakeet?" Ryan asked.

"Not exactly."

The twins hadn't heard anything about a bird.

The yard was set up with tables for a cookout. Bobby's dad was grilling. Bobby decided to pretend that he didn't know there was an eagle in his future.

Mrs. Quinn called everyone to come and eat. Bobby had one hot dog and one hamburger and lots of chips. He didn't think he had room for cake. Then his father carried out a big square cake. It had chocolate frosting and the words Happy Birthday Bobby.

Bobby ate two pieces of cake, one with ice cream.

Finally, Bobby's father said, "It's time to open the presents."

Bobby felt his stomach go up and down. Maybe it was all that food. Or maybe it was the thought of getting an eagle. He tried to practice making a surprised face. A happy, surprised face.

"Are you all right, Bobby?" his father asked. "You look so strange."

"No, no, Dad. I'm okay."

"Then let's open presents," Mr. Quinn said.

Bobby got lots of nice presents. There was the dinosaur book from Brian and Ryan. His grandparents in Florida sent a check. Jenny's family gave him a paint set.

Bobby's mother smiled. "Now it's time for your special present," she said.

His father said, "Close your eyes."

Bobby was glad to close his eyes. It would be easier to look surprised when he opened them.

"Okay, Bobby," his father called, "you can look!"

Bobby opened his eyes. He didn't have to pretend to be surprised. Or happy. In his father's arms was a puppy. The cutest, squirmiest little dog Bobby had ever seen.

Bobby reached out for the puppy. "It's… It's…"

"It's a beagle," his father finished for

him. "A five-month-old beagle puppy."

Bobby took the puppy. He whispered in the dog's ear. "You're not an eagle. You're a beagle."

He turned the puppy around and looked her in the eyes. "Absolutely the prettiest beagle in the whole world!"

Lucy

"When are you going to name your dog?" Bobby's mother asked.

Bobby was sitting at the kitchen table. The puppy bit at his shoe. "I have to find just the right name," he told her.

"But it's been three days," his mother said. "We can't start training the puppy until we name her. What about Snoopy? The beagle in the Peanuts cartoon is named Snoopy."

Bobby shook his head. There was already one dog named Snoopy. Why have another one?

Bobby wanted a name that was special.

"How about Rover?" his mother asked as she started lunch. "Or King?"

"She's a girl, Mom," Bobby said.

"Right. Then what about Queenie? Or Princess?" Mrs. Quinn suggested.

Bobby shook his head.

Bobby's father came into the kitchen. "I have a name," he said.

Bobby looked up.

"Trey. It's another word for three," Mr. Quinn told Bobby. "The puppy has three colors. She's mostly white, but she has streaks of brown and bits of black."

"Trey," Bobby said. He looked into the puppy's eyes. They were the color of dark chocolate. "Hi, Trey," he called.

The little beagle gave Bobby a funny look. "Nope," Bobby said. "That's not it."

His father sighed. "Well, try to come

up with something pretty soon."

Bobby picked up his puppy and a library book about beagles. He went outside. The backyard had a fence around it, so the dog could not run away. He put his puppy down and looked through the book.

Bobby had read this book three times since he checked it out of the library. He had learned a lot about beagles. He learned they were dogs that liked to run and chase. They could be wild. They were also dogs that liked to chew. This puppy had already chewed up the wrappings from Bobby's presents.

Bobby closed the book. He watched the dog as she ran around the yard. She was not a shy dog. She loved running up to people. She thought everyone was her friend.

This puppy reminded him of his favorite babysitter, Lucy. Bobby was very sad when she moved away.

Lucy was always happy to see him. She had lots of friends. Sometimes, she took Bobby to the park. They would see other children there. He would try to hide behind her. But Lucy would just whisper in his ear, "You are a great kid." Then she would take him by the hand to meet the other children.

Bobby didn't feel so shy when he was with Lucy.

Lucy. That would be a perfect name for the puppy. The dog was pretty like Lucy, and brave, and fun. Yes, he would name his beagle Lucy.

Bobby tried it out. "Come here, Lucy."

Lucy stopped running.

"Lucy, girl. Come here."

The puppy bounded over to Bobby. Bobby picked her up, and she started licking his face.

"Okay. Okay." Bobby laughed. "I get it. You like the name Lucy."

Lucy stopped licking. She looked right at Bobby and nodded her head. That's what it looked like, anyway.

"Wow, Lucy!" Bobby said. "You already know your name."

Was he lucky or what? Lucy was smart. Lucy was beautiful. Lucy could understand human talk. And most of all, Lucy liked him. Lucy wasn't just the best dog in the world. She was his friend.

Lucy in Trouble

Lucy may have been the best dog in the world, but she wasn't the easiest dog to live with.

She liked to howl. She liked to run. She liked to chew. She LOVED to chew.

One morning, Bobby's mother asked, "Has anybody seen my slipper?"

Bobby had seen it. It was at the foot of his bed. A brown, fleecy slipper all curled up in a ball, looking like a mouse. It made Bobby jump when he saw it.

"I think Lucy got hold of your slipper," Bobby told her.

His mom sighed. "Puppies like to chew.

I should have been more careful. From now on, let's put the things she might like to chew out of sight."

The family tried. Mrs. Quinn gave Lucy her other slipper. "Chew away, Lucy," she said. Then she moved the rest of her shoes to a shelf in the closet. She put her magazines on a table.

Bobby tried to make sure his clothes were picked up. He didn't always remember. He remembered better after Lucy chewed a hole through his favorite Chicago Cubs T-shirt.

Mr. Quinn hung up all his clothes. He put his dirty socks in the hamper. He put his slippers on his night table.

"See?" he bragged. "It's not hard to keep Lucy away from things. You just have to be careful. Like me."

One hot evening, Mr. Quinn came home after work. He was tired and sweaty. He tossed a folder onto the sofa.

"What's that?" Bobby's mother asked.

"Some papers I have to read. I have a big meeting in the morning."

"Do it after dinner," Mrs. Quinn told him. "It's almost time to eat."

Bobby was slurping spaghetti when he heard another sound. It came from the living room. It was a tearing, ripping sound. Bobby looked up. His mother and father heard it, too. There was one more noise. Growling.

"I moved all the magazines," Mrs. Quinn said.

"It must be..." Mr. Quinn jumped up. Mrs. Quinn and Bobby hurried to follow him.

The living room was covered with pieces of paper. They were the important papers that Mr. Quinn had brought home with him. Some of them were torn. Some were chewed. Lucy was pawing and biting a piece of yellow paper.

"Oh, no!" Mr. Quinn moaned.

Mrs. Quinn rushed to pick up the papers. Bobby grabbed Lucy up in his arms. She wriggled to get free.

"No, Lucy. Chewing those papers was a bad thing to do."

Lucy looked around. She watched Mr. Quinn rubbing his hand through his hair and Mrs. Quinn gathering papers. Lucy seemed to know she had made a big mess of things. She hung her head.

"You can still read them," Mrs. Quinn said. She picked up a piece of paper with

a big hole in the middle. "Well, maybe not this one."

"It was my fault," Mr. Quinn said. "I shouldn't have left the folder on the sofa." He still looked mad.

Lucy wriggled out of Bobby's arms. She trotted over to Mr. Quinn. He was now down on his knees, helping his wife pick up the papers. Lucy licked his hand.

"Lucy, are you trying to make up with me?" Mr. Quinn tried to keep a stern look on his face. Lucy licked his hand again.

Mr. Quinn had to smile. "It's very hard to stay mad at you. Almost as hard as keeping things out of your way." He rubbed the dog's head.

Lucy jumped up and down, happy again.

"What are you going to do?" Mrs.

Quinn asked her husband.

"I guess I'll read what I can," Mr. Quinn replied as he stood up. He started laughing.

"What's so funny?" Bobby asked.

"When I was about your age, I once forgot to do my homework. So I told the teacher my dog ate it."

"You did?" Bobby's eyes were wide.

"My teacher didn't believe me." Mr. Quinn laughed harder. "I wonder if my boss will believe me when I tell him that your dog ate my homework!"

5

Lucy to the Rescue

The month of July was hot. Bobby's mother said it was hot enough to fry an egg on the sidewalk. But when Bobby asked her for an egg, she just glared at him. The hot weather was putting everyone in a bad mood.

Bobby looked out his living room window. He could see the children who had moved in across the street. There was a boy who was younger than Bobby, a girl who was older than Bobby, and another boy just about Bobby's age. The children were playing volleyball. The girl and the little boy were one team. The other boy was a team all by himself. He was good at hitting the ball over the net.

The game looked like fun. Bobby wished he could be playing with the new kids. Then he thought about going across the street and saying hello. He knew he absolutely could not do it.

Meeting new people made his heart pound fast. His face got red. Even his ears got red. He was afraid he'd do something stupid. No, it was better not to try and meet new people. Anyway, now that he had Lucy, he didn't need any other friends.

Lucy woke up from her nap. She danced around Bobby.

"Do you want to go for a walk?" Bobby asked.

What if they went for a walk and those

kids across the street tried to talk to him? What would he say?

"Are you sure you want to go?" Bobby asked Lucy.

Lucy kept on dancing.

"All right. I'll get your leash."

Bobby and Lucy went outside. Bobby snuck a look across the street. The children were gone.

Bobby and Lucy walked down the street. No one was around. Maybe everyone was inside, trying to keep cool.

The house on the corner was big and yellow. Old Mr. Davis lived in the house. Sometimes Bobby saw him bringing in his newspaper or weeding his garden. His garden was full of roses, day lilies, and big sunflowers that were taller than Bobby.

Mr. Davis was sitting in a rocking chair

on his porch. When Bobby and Lucy walked past, Mr. Davis lifted his hand.

"Hi, Bobby," he said in a tired voice. "What's your dog's name?"

"Lucy." Bobby could feel his face starting to get red.

Lucy stood up on her hind legs and barked at the sound of her name. Bobby hurried on.

On the next block was a small park. It was mostly for little kids. The children went on the swings or played in the sandbox. Today the park was empty except for a toddler and his babysitter.

The boy was taking fast baby steps on his chubby legs. He looked like he might tumble over, but he never did.

The boy started to cry when he saw Lucy. His babysitter picked him up.

"I guess he's afraid of dogs," the girl said.

Bobby didn't see how anybody could be afraid of Lucy. "She's nice. She likes everybody," Bobby said.

"Do you want to say hello to the doggie?" the babysitter asked the boy.

He shook his head no.

"I'm sorry," the babysitter said to Bobby. "Would you mind taking your dog to the other side of the park?"

Bobby felt bad that the boy didn't like Lucy. But he did what the babysitter asked. He and Lucy walked away.

Bobby sat on a park bench. He tossed a stick to Lucy.

"Fetch, Lucy," Bobby said. He wanted to see if she would bring it back to him. She didn't.

He looked over at the little boy. Too bad he wouldn't give Lucy a chance. But Bobby knew it was hard to give something new a chance.

It was too hot to stay in the park for long. Slowly Bobby and Lucy walked home.

Mr. Davis was still sitting in his chair, but now his eyes were closed. *He must be sleeping,* Bobby thought. He was ready to walk by, but Lucy stopped and stood very still.

"What's wrong?" Bobby wanted to go home and have a cool drink.

Lucy wouldn't move. She stared at Mr. Davis. Then she pulled hard on her leash. She wanted to go up on Mr. Davis's porch.

"No, Lucy," Bobby said.

But Lucy wouldn't take no for an

answer. She kept tugging on her leash. Finally, Bobby followed her up the stairs.

Mr. Davis was sweating. His eyes were still closed.

"Mr. Davis?" Bobby said softly.

Mr. Davis didn't answer.

Bobby felt scared. "Are you okay?" he asked. "Mr. Davis, can you hear me?"

Mr. Davis's eyes fluttered. "Bobby?"

"Are you okay?" Bobby asked again.

"Bobby, go get your mother," Mr. Davis said in a weak voice. "I don't feel very good."

Bobby and Lucy ran all the way home.

6
One Friend

Bobby's mother raced over to Mr. Davis's house. Bobby and Lucy were right behind her.

Mr. Davis was breathing hard. "My medicine," he gasped. "It's on the kitchen table."

Bobby had never seen his mother move so fast. She brought out the medicine and a glass of water. She helped Mr. Davis take his medicine.

"I'll be better in a minute or two," Mr. Davis said.

"I'm going to call 911," Mrs. Quinn said.

"No, no. The medicine works fast," he told her. "Take me into the house."

Mrs. Quinn helped Mr. Davis inside. He sat on the couch. He was starting to look better.

"Sorry," Mr. Davis said. "I didn't mean to scare anybody. I was so tired, I couldn't get inside to get my medicine."

Mrs. Quinn turned to Bobby. "How did you know Mr. Davis was sick?"

"I didn't," Bobby said. "It was Lucy."

"Lucy!" his mother exclaimed.

"She knew something was wrong," Bobby told her. "She wouldn't go home until we checked on Mr. Davis."

Mr. Davis was sitting up straighter. "That little dog is a hero," he said.

Bobby looked down at Lucy, who was sitting quietly at his feet.

"Wow, Lucy. You're a hero."

Mrs. Quinn gave Lucy a pat. "I should say so," she said. "Mr. Davis, how are you feeling now?"

Mr. Davis took a deep breath. "Just about back to normal."

"Can I call someone for you?" Mrs. Quinn asked Mr. Davis.

"My daughter, maybe," he replied.

Bobby and his mother said they would wait with Mr. Davis until his daughter came over.

Mr. Davis had a very interesting house. Pictures of soldiers and cowboys were on the walls. Two big fish hung on the wall, too. Mr. Davis told Bobby he caught those fish when he was a boy.

The other things that filled the house were books, books, and more books. Some were in bookshelves. Some were on tables. There were piles of books on the floor. Bobby liked the book of Bible stories with shiny colored pictures.

Mr. Davis's daughter made a fuss when she came. She thanked Bobby and his mother over and over. She thanked Lucy, too. Mr. Davis told Bobby to come by anytime.

The next day was hotter than the one before. Bobby was bored.

"Mom, will you take me to a movie?" he asked.

"I'm busy paying bills. Maybe later."

Then Bobby had an idea.

"Do you think I should go to Mr. Davis's house?" Bobby asked.

Mrs. Quinn looked up at him. "Do you want to?"

"His house had lots of neat stuff," Bobby told her. "And he told me to come over anytime."

"Yes, he did," his mother agreed.

"I could see if he's feeling better today," Bobby said.

"It would be very nice of you to visit Mr. Davis," Bobby's mother said.

"Okay. Lucy and I will go."

Bobby put Lucy on her leash, and they walked down the street. The closer they got to the yellow house, the louder Bobby's heart bumped. It was one thing to help Mr. Davis when he was sick. It was another thing to stop by for a visit.

"Maybe we should just go home," Bobby whispered to Lucy.

But Lucy pulled Bobby forward. Mr. Davis was working in his yard.

"Hello, there!" Mr. Davis called. "I'm feeling fine today. Did you come by to say hello?"

Lucy hurried toward the gate. Bobby had to run to keep up with her.

"Yes," Bobby said. There was no turning back now.

"My daughter brought me some cookies and lemonade this morning," Mr. Davis said as they climbed the stairs. "Would you like some?"

Bobby nodded. Bobby, Mr. Davis, and Lucy went inside. Mr. Davis got the lemonade and cookies. Bobby looked at a picture of a cowboy on the wall.

"That was my grandfather," Mr. Davis said.

"Your grandfather was a cowboy?" Bobby asked with surprise.

"He was a cowboy in Texas after the Civil War." He pointed to another picture. "That's him when he was a soldier."

"Wow," Bobby said. "A cowboy and a soldier. All my grandfather does is work in a grocery store."

"Would you like me to tell you about my grandfather?" Mr. Davis asked.

"Sure," Bobby said.

Mr. Davis sat on the couch. Bobby sat next to him. Lucy snuggled between them. Mr. Davis opened a photo album that was on the table. "Now this is a picture of my grandfather when he was a boy in Ohio," Mr. Davis began. "That little fellow with him is his friend from the next farm. They were friends for their whole lives. They even went to Texas together when they were grown up."

Bobby liked listening to Mr. Davis's stories. He especially liked the stories about the two young friends.

Bobby looked over at Mr. Davis. Bobby thought maybe now he had a friend. White hair. Lots of wrinkles. Old. But a friend.

7

Dog School

"School!" Bobby exclaimed. "Mom, Lucy doesn't want to go to school!"

Bobby's mother looked out the kitchen window at Lucy. Lucy was digging a hole in Mrs. Quinn's garden. It was the third time this week.

"Bobby," Mrs. Quinn said, "Lucy needs to go to obedience school."

"She does what I tell her. Let's go outside. I'll show you."

Bobby and his mother went outside. Lucy was still busy digging.

"Lucy, come. Come here, girl."

Lucy didn't even look up.

"Lucy," Bobby called again.

This time Lucy did lift her head. Then she went back to digging.

Bobby went over to Lucy and picked her up. She squirmed.

"Okay, try this." Bobby put Lucy down on the ground. "Sit, Lucy. Sit."

Lucy looked at Bobby.

"Sit."

Lucy lowered her tail down to the ground. She almost sat down. But she didn't. Her tail started wagging. She jumped up. Then she ran around in a circle trying to catch her tail.

"See what I mean?" Bobby's mother asked. "Lucy needs to learn to sit. She needs to learn to stand quietly. She needs to learn how to obey."

"But it's summer," Bobby complained.

"Nobody should have to go to school in the summer."

"The summer is a perfect time for a dog to go to school," Mrs. Quinn said. "Obedience classes are starting in the park. I think we should sign up Lucy."

That night they talked about obedience school with Bobby's father. He thought sending Lucy to school was a very good idea.

"Maybe Lucy will learn to like her leash," Mr. Quinn said.

Lucy didn't like being on her leash at all. Lucy liked to run free. Bobby didn't think there was a school in the world that could make Lucy like her leash.

"Who will take Lucy to this school?" Bobby asked.

His parents looked at each other.

"Why don't you and I take her, Bobby?" his father asked.

Bobby didn't like this idea at all. It was bad enough Lucy had to go to school. He didn't want to go to school, too. School meant new people to meet. New people he would have to talk to.

"Can I think about it?" Bobby asked.

"Yes, think about it, Bobby," said his mother. "But don't take too long. Lots of people want to sign their dogs up for obedience school."

The next day, Bobby and Lucy went to visit Mr. Davis. Bobby told Mr. Davis about obedience school.

"But why don't you want to go?" Mr. Davis asked.

Bobby could feel his face get red. "Too many new people," he mumbled.

"Are you shy, Bobby?" Mr. Davis asked with surprise.

"I guess," Bobby said in a quiet voice.

"Really? You don't seem like a shy boy to me."

Now it was Bobby's turn to be surprised. "I don't?"

"Not at all," Mr. Davis said.

Bobby was glad he didn't seem like a shy boy to Mr. Davis.

Mr. Davis poured some lemonade into Bobby's glass.

"Bobby, what about Lucy?" he asked.

"What about her?"

"Do you think she needs to go to obedience school?" Mr. Davis asked.

Bobby had to be honest. "Yes."

"You are her owner," Mr. Davis reminded him. "Don't you think you should be with her at school?"

"My dad could take her."

"Would that be the same?" Mr. Davis asked. "I think Lucy would like to have you there with her."

Lucy was sitting next to Bobby. She gave a long, low howl.

Bobby had to laugh. "Yes. I guess she would."

"You never can tell, Bobby," Mr. Davis said. "Maybe obedience school will be fun."

Fun? Bobby didn't think so. But if Lucy had to go to obedience school, Bobby was going with her. Lucy needed him.

8

Two Friends

Big dogs. Little dogs. Furry dogs. Sleek dogs. Mighty dogs and mutts. Dogs were walking, running, barking, and yapping all over the park.

It was the first day of obedience school.

Lucy trotted to the edge of the grass. Then she stopped and looked up at Bobby.

"She's never seen so many dogs," Bobby said to his father.

"I think there are only about ten dogs," Mr. Quinn said. "It just seems like more because they are so noisy."

"How is Lucy going to learn to be obedient when all these dogs are so wild?" Bobby asked.

"The dogs will learn to be obedient together," Mr. Quinn said. But he didn't look all that sure.

A chunky woman with curly hair and a big smile said hello. She wore a big, shiny silver whistle around her neck.

"I'm Marsha. I'm the trainer," she said.

Mr. Quinn introduced himself. He introduced Bobby and Lucy.

Marsha leaned over and patted Lucy's head. "Hello, Lucy. You're going to be a good student, aren't you?"

Lucy tried to jump on Marsha and lick her face.

Marsha just laughed. "We'll start in a few minutes. When I blow my whistle, meet me by the big oak tree."

Marsha pointed out the tree. Then she walked away.

"She seems nice," Mr. Quinn said.

"Lucy liked her," Bobby said.

"Hi," said a girl about Bobby's age.

Bobby looked at the ground. "Hi," he mumbled.

"My name is Candy," the girl said. "This is Butch." She pointed to her dog, a boxer.

Mr. Quinn patted Butch on the head. "Hello, Butch. Hello, Candy. I'm Mr. Quinn, and this is Bobby."

Butch sniffed at Lucy. Lucy sniffed right back.

"How long have you had Lucy?" Candy asked.

Before Bobby could answer, Candy said, "We've had Butch about two months.

We got him from a neighbor who was moving away. His name was already Butch. He looks like a Butch, don't you think? Is Lucy a good dog?"

Bobby looked at his father. Bobby hoped he would answer all the girl's questions.

"What about it, Bobby?" Mr. Quinn asked. "Is Lucy a good dog?"

"Yes," Bobby said quietly.

"Butch isn't," Candy told Bobby.

Butch gave a long growl.

"Butch is wild," Candy looked rather happy about that fact. "My mother says Butch is driving her crazy."

Candy's mother joined the group. "That's why Butch is going to obedience school," she said.

Marsha blew her whistle. Dogs and

their owners gathered by the big oak tree.

"Go ahead, Bobby," his father said.

"What about you?" Bobby asked.

"I'll wait on the sidelines and watch," his father answered.

"I thought we were going to do this together. You, me, and Lucy."

"No," Mr. Quinn said. "A dog needs one person to train with."

Candy tugged at Bobby's arm. "C'mon, let's go."

Bobby looked back at his father as Candy dragged him away. His father just gave him a wave.

Everyone was lining up with their dogs.

"I think our dogs are the best, don't you?" Candy asked.

Bobby looked at the other dogs. It was hard to judge. All the dogs were so

different. He thought Lucy was the best. He wasn't too sure about Butch.

"Lucy and Butch are the best, right?" Candy asked again.

Butch looked like he might be the best at growling. He was growling loudly at the other dogs. Candy was still waiting for an answer.

"I guess our dogs are the best," Bobby finally said.

Candy said, "I like having a big dog. The other day Butch…"

Candy sure liked to talk, Bobby thought to himself.

Marsha blew her whistle again. "We will begin by teaching our dogs how to come when we call their names. Dogs want to learn to obey their masters. It makes them happy. It makes us happy."

For the next half hour, the owners called their dogs. When they came, the owners patted their pets and said, "Good dog."

By the end of the class, Lucy was coming when Bobby called her.

Butch was another story. Sometimes Butch ran away when Candy called him. Sometimes he sat down and scratched himself. Every once in a while, when he felt like it, Butch came.

"He's getting the hang of it. Don't you think so?" Candy asked Bobby when the class was over.

Bobby didn't want to hurt Candy's feelings. "Well, he's trying," Bobby said.

Bobby picked up Lucy. He looked around for his father.

"Let's go get ice cream," Candy said.

"What?" Bobby asked with surprise. No one his age had ever asked him to go for ice cream.

"We worked hard. Let's get some ice cream," Candy repeated.

"I—I don't think I can," Bobby said.

"Why not?" Candy wanted to know.

Bobby's father and Candy's mother found them.

"Good job, Lucy." Mr. Quinn gave Lucy a pat. "Ready to go, Bobby?"

"I asked Bobby to go get ice cream with us. Is that okay, Mom?"

"I don't see why not," Candy's mother said. "Bobby doesn't live too far from us. We can take him home."

"That sounds like a good idea," Mr. Quinn said. "I'll take Lucy with me."

No one had asked Bobby if he wanted

to go. He didn't want to go. He felt shy just thinking about it.

"I'm going to have Rocky Road ice cream," Candy said. "What kind do you like, Bobby?"

Before Bobby could answer, Candy said, "I bet you like chocolate. Maybe we can get banana splits. What about it, Mom?"

Mr. Quinn and Lucy left. Bobby found himself walking out of the park with Candy, her mother, and Butch.

They went to the ice cream shop. Candy had a banana split. Bobby had a double dip cone. Chocolate.

Bobby and Candy sat outside the shop eating their ice cream.

Candy said, "I'm going to work with Butch all week until he comes when I call him. He's very smart. He's just not trying."

Candy giggled. "That's what my teacher says about me sometimes. Maybe you should come over to my house with Lucy. We can practice together. Saturday would be a good day. You can come over in the afternoon."

The worst thing about being shy was never knowing what to say next. Bobby could see this wasn't going to be a problem with Candy. She talked enough for both of them.

"Will you come?" Candy asked.

Bobby licked his ice cream cone. It tasted great.

"Yes, I'll come. Absolutely."

9

One More Friend

Now Bobby had two friends. And what a surprise! His friends were an elderly man and a girl. Even so, Mr. Davis and Candy made very good friends. It was easy to be around them. He had fun with them. They made him laugh. Sometimes, he even made them laugh.

Lucy and Butch had been going to obedience school for three weeks. Lucy came when she was called. She would sit. She would fetch a ball. Butch would not fetch a ball. He would not sit. He still answered to his name only when he felt like it.

One day in August, Bobby and Candy

were sitting on Bobby's porch. Butch and Lucy were sleeping at their feet.

"My mom's getting kind of mad at Butch," Candy said. "She doesn't think he's trying very hard."

Bobby thought maybe Candy's mother was right.

"I told her Butch is trying. Maybe he's just dumb."

Butch must have heard this. He opened his eyes and growled.

"Sorry, Butch," Candy said. Butch closed his eyes and fell back asleep. "We're going to miss two classes while we are away. Mom says I can use the time to practice stuff Butch hasn't learned yet."

"You're going away?" Bobby asked. This was the first he had heard about Candy going somewhere.

"Oh, yes. We're going to the lake for two weeks," Candy told Bobby. "We're going to stay in a cottage."

Bobby had a funny feeling in his stomach. He wasn't sure what the feeling was. Then it hit him. He was feeling funny because he was going to miss Candy. He had never missed a friend before.

The day Candy left, Bobby was lonely. He decided to take Lucy for a walk and visit Mr. Davis. But when they got to the yellow house, Mr. Davis was locking his door. He was carrying a small suitcase.

"Are you going somewhere?" Bobby asked.

"Yes, Bobby," Mr. Davis said. "I'm going to stay with my daughter for a while."

"Are you feeling all right?"

"Don't worry. I'm fine," Mr. Davis answered. "But my house is so hot. I have just the one small air conditioner in the bedroom. My daughter's whole house is air conditioned. I'm going to stay there until it gets cooler."

"Oh." Bobby had that funny feeling in his stomach again.

Mr. Davis looked at Bobby. "I won't be gone very long. As soon as we get a good, cool breeze, you look for me."

"Have a good time," Bobby said in a small voice.

Lucy yipped. It seemed like Lucy knew that Mr. Davis was leaving, too.

A car honked.

"There's my daughter," Mr. Davis said. He hurried down the stairs. "See you, Bobby. Bye, Lucy."

Bobby sat down on Mr. Davis's rocking chair. He picked up Lucy and put her on his lap. There was that funny feeling again. He was lonesome. He missed his friends.

One day passed. Then another and another. Bobby wasn't just lonesome anymore. He was bored. Bobby was *so* bored.

He spent most of his time watching television.

"Do you want to go to the library and get some books?" his mother asked.

"No. It's too hot to read."

His mother frowned. "It may be too hot to play ball, but it's never too hot to read."

Bobby was grumpy. "I just don't feel like reading."

"Do you want to go to the swimming pool later?" his mother asked. "That would cool you off."

Bobby shrugged. "I don't care."

Now his mother was getting mad. She said, "Bobby, all you do is watch TV. At least take Lucy for a walk."

Bobby looked at Lucy. Lucy was stretched out in front of the air conditioning vent. She did not look like she wanted to go anywhere. Then Bobby looked at his mother. She did not look like she was going to take no for an answer. So Bobby got up and clipped Lucy's leash on her.

"We might melt," Bobby warned his mother.

"If you don't come back, I'll look for two puddles of water—one with a tail floating in it." Mrs. Quinn was smiling.

Bobby and Lucy went outside. He glanced at the house across the street. He hadn't seen the new kids in a long time. Maybe they were on vacation like Candy.

Then Bobby saw someone coming out of the house. It was the boy who was about his own age. The boy began bouncing a yellow tennis ball. He acted like he didn't know Lucy and Bobby were across the street. But Bobby could see him peeking at them about every third bounce.

Should I say hi? Bobby wondered. He could feel his face getting red, and it wasn't just from the heat. He was being shy again. Maybe he had two friends now. But he still didn't want to go up to a strange kid and say hello. Bobby walked more quickly down the block.

Suddenly, Lucy stopped. She had spotted something. The yellow tennis ball was rolling in her direction.

Lucy knew what to do. She had done it plenty of times at obedience school. She tugged at her leash so she could fetch the ball. She grabbed it with her mouth as it rolled by. She tugged on her leash. She tried to get Bobby to cross the street. She wanted to give the ball back to the boy.

Bobby didn't want to go across the street. But Lucy did.

The boy was in no hurry to get his ball. He just stood there as Bobby and Lucy came toward him. His eyes were down on the sidewalk.

He's not very friendly, Bobby thought. Then Bobby realized that he knew that look. He knew it very well. It wasn't the look of someone who was unfriendly. It was the look of someone who was shy.

Lucy scampered up to the boy. She

dropped the ball at his feet and gave a happy bark.

"Can you give her a pat for bringing you the ball?" Bobby asked. "That's what they tell us to do at obedience school."

The boy didn't say anything, but he patted Lucy's head.

Lucy pushed the ball with her paw.

The boy looked up. "What's her name?" the boy asked in a small voice.

"Lucy. What's your name?" Bobby asked boldly.

"Shawn."

"I'm Bobby. I live across the street."

"I know," Shawn said. "I've seen you. She looks like a great dog."

"She is," Bobby said.

"My mom won't let me get a dog yet." Shawn smiled. "But I'm working on her."

"Dogs make great friends," Bobby told him.

"I'll tell my mother that," Shawn said.

Neither boy said anything for a few seconds.

Bobby felt uncomfortable. That's how he felt when he couldn't think of anything to say to the kids at school. Bobby thought maybe it was time to go.

But Lucy had other ideas. She picked up the ball in her mouth. She looked first at Bobby, then at Shawn.

"She wants to play," Bobby said. He took the ball from Lucy's mouth. Then he took a great big breath. "We have a fenced-in yard for Lucy. Do you want to come to my house and play with her?"

Shawn looked happy. "I'll go ask my mother," he said. "I'll be right back."

Bobby sat down on the grass to wait for Shawn. He pulled Lucy close to him.

"Lucy," he whispered, "I have a feeling Shawn might be my third friend. Wow," he continued softly, "three friends."

He thought about how he had met each of his friends. He met all of them because of Lucy. Lucy was like a lucky charm.

Bobby gave his dog a squeeze.

"Even if I make a hundred friends," he told her, "you will always be my best friend. You are absolutely the best dog in the world. Absolutely, Lucy."

Lucy barked. She agreed.

Read the next books about Lucy!

Lucy on the Loose

"Ben!" Shawn said. "What happened to Lucy?"

"She . . . she ran away!" Ben said in a shaky voice.

Bobby jumped up. "Ran away? Where?"

"That way." Ben was confused. He pointed in one direction. "Or maybe that way." He pointed in the other direction.

"Which way was it?" Shawn demanded.

"I'm not sure." Ben was almost crying. "But she was chasing a big orange C-A-T!"

Look at Lucy!

On the way out, a large, colorful poster taller than the boys caught Bobby's eye.

The poster had a drawing of different kinds of animals crowded together in front of a television camera. Across the top were the words WANTED: SPOKESPET FOR PET-O-RAMA! Under the picture of the animals it said, "Is your pet cute? Smart? Funny? Enter the Pet-O-Rama spokespet contest and your pet could be on TV!"

Bobby read the poster carefully. Cute, smart, funny? That described Lucy! She could win the spokespet contest, easy!